MUIZENBERG

KALK BAY

FISHHOEK

GLENCAIRN

SIMONSTOWN

MILLERS POINT

SMITSWINKEL BAY

BUFFELS BAAI

FALSE BAY

INDIAN OCEAN

5.

6.

SILVER MINE NATURE RESERVE

CAPE POINT NATURE RESERVE

VOORDHOEK

MASIPHUMELELE

WITSAND

SCARBOROUGH

ATLANTIC OCEAN

PLATBOOMBAAI

CAPE OF GOOD HOPE

CAPE POINT

CAPE PENINSULA

N NE E SE S SW W NW

D0943066

First published in South Africa in **2013**
by Bumble Books, an imprint of Publishing Print Matters (Pty) Ltd
6 Opal way, San Michel, Noordhoek 7979
Western Cape, South Africa
www.printmatters.co.za
info@printmatters.co.za

A CIP catalogue record for this book is available at the South African Library.

ISBN: 978-0-9802610-3-5

Printed and Bound by
Creda communications,
Cape Town.

bumble books

FOR:

Kambani, a true friend ...

lion's Head

... and for the lovely tea ladies.

* The publisher & the author would like to thank the following subscribers, & those wishing to remain anonymous, for their generous support of the printing of this book:

Air Films, Charlotte & Ivan Beck, Valda & Henk Beets, The Bright Foundation, Kathy & Eddie Drummer, Claerwen Howie, Marge Hughes, The Humbert Family Trust, Des & Marsalidh Kilalea, Libri Tortilis, Kirsty Macfarlane, The Maclons Clan, The Page-Muller Family, Mathilda Noluthando Perrill-Estoppey, Charlotte Stuart-Clark, Elizabeth Stuart-Clark, Dr Hannah Stuart-Clark, Jane Stuart-Clark, & The Torres Family.

TABLE MOUNTAIN'S HOLIDAY

Written & Illustrated by

Lucy Stuart-Clark.

& Table Mountain.

bumble books

Tired of being covered by a cold,
cloudy blanket, Table Mountain
        stretches his reptilian legs,
    waves good-bye to Lion's Head ...

... ~~and~~ & goes on holiday!

He feeds ~~squirrels~~ squirrels in the Company Gardens ...

& cucumber
Sand#wiches

... & has tea^ at the Mount Nelson Hotel ...

... before ~~a~~ catching a _boat_ ~~the ferry~~ to Robben Island.

He watches a movie at the Waterfront
& then does a bit of shopping ...

really

... but ~~really~~ doesn't enjoy either.

(it was too crowded, too small!)

So, he spends some time cooling his feet
in Muizenberg ...

... and tries ~~A~~ shark-cage diving
in False Bay.

Dearest Leo,

I am having such a wonderful
holiday, but miss you terribly.
The seagulls are much friendlier
at the Indian Ocean than they are
at home ... I think it must have
something to do with the warmer
currents ... &, of course, tourists
being distracted from their fish
& chips while whale -
spotting!   see you soon!!

T.M
xxx (P.S THE MOUNT NELSON HOTEL
MAKES A VERY GOOD
CUCUMBER
SANDWICH)

South Africa standard postage

MAIL
2011 07 01

LION'S HEAD

~~NEXT TO TABLE~~

~~MOUNTAIN~~

(ASK A SEAGULL)

CRUMB

When the South-easter blows across
the peninsula ~~too strongly~~ a little too strongly
he decides to stay indoors for a few days ...

... and then wanders into the Karoo
for a spot of star-gazing ...

(which I particularly
enjoyed!)

Best

,... but, missing his ^friend,
Table Mountain soon decides that
it is time to go home .

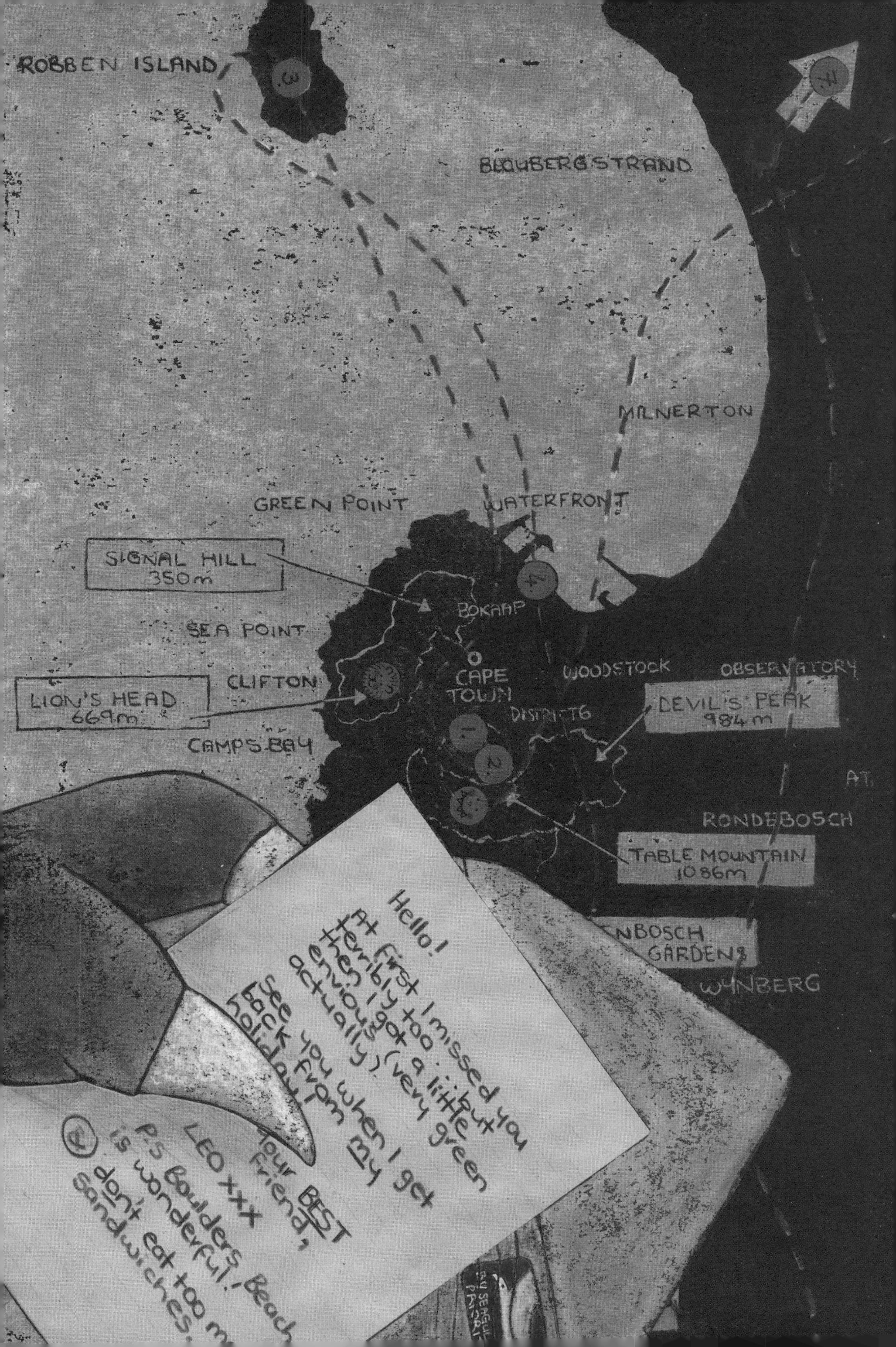
ROBBEN ISLAND
BLOUBERGSTRAND
MILNERTON
GREEN POINT
WATERFRONT
SIGNAL HILL 350m
BOKAAP
SEA POINT
CLIFTON
CAPE TOWN
LION'S HEAD 669m
CAMPS BAY
WOODSTOCK
OBSERVATORY
DEVIL'S PEAK 984m
DISTRICT 6
RONDEBOSCH
TABLE MOUNTAIN 1086m
NBOSCH GARDENS
WYNBERG
Hello!
At first I missed you terribly too ... but then I got a little envious (very green actually).
See you when I get back from my holiday!
Your BEST friend,
LEO xxx
P.S Boulders Beach is wonderful!
& don't eat too m
sandwiches.